Copyright © 1985 by Nord-Süd Verlag, Mönchaltorf, Switzerland
First published in Switzerland under the title *Die Sterntaler*
English translation copyright © 1985 by Abelard-Schuman Ltd
North-South Books English language edition copyright © 1985 by
Rada Matija AG, 8625 Gossau ZH, Switzerland

10 9 8 7 6 5

First published in the United States, Great Britain, Canada,
Australia and New Zealand in 1985 by North-South Books,
an imprint of Rada Matija AG

Library of Congress Cataloging in Publication Data

Grimm, Wilhelm, 1786–1859
  The falling stars.
  Summary: A poor child who possesses nothing but the
clothes on her back gives everything away to others who
are suffering and receives a reward from the heavens.
  [1. Fairy tales. 2. Folklore – Germany] I. Grimm,
Jacob, 1785–1863. II. Sopko, Eugen ill. III. Title.
PZ8.G883Fal   1985   398.2'1'0943   85-7193
ISBN 1-55858-041-7

British Library Cataloguing in Publication Data

Grimm, Jacob
  The falling stars.
  I. Title II. Grimm, Wilhelm III. Sopko,
  Eugen IV. Die Sterntaler, *English*
  398.2'1'0943   PT2281.G2/
ISBN 1-55858-041-7

THE BROTHERS GRIMM

THE FALLING STARS

Illustrated by
Eugen Sopko

Translated by
Rosemary Lanning

North-South Books
New York

There was once a little girl whose mother and father died and left her with nothing – nowhere to live, not even a little bed to sleep in.

She had nothing but the clothes she was wearing and a small piece of bread which a kind ~~soul~~ *person* had given her, but in spite of everything she was a sweet and gentle child.

Because there was no one to care for her she put all her trust in God and went out into the world.

First she met a poor man who said, "I'm so hungry. Please give me something to eat!"

The little girl gave him all her bread. "Take this, with God's blessing," she said.

Then she walked on.

Next she met a crying child. "My head is so cold," said the child. "Please give me something to keep it warm!" So she took off her cap and gave it away.

And when she had gone a little further she met another child, shivering with cold because he had no jacket. So she gave him her jacket.

Still further on she met another child asking for a
skirt, and again she gave her own skirt away.

Finally she came to a forest. Night had already fallen when she met another child who asked for her shirt. "The night is dark," thought the little girl. "No one will see me. I don't need my shirt." She took it off and gave it away. And as she stood there, with nothing left at all, stars suddenly began to fall from the sky, and as they fell they turned into shining gold coins.

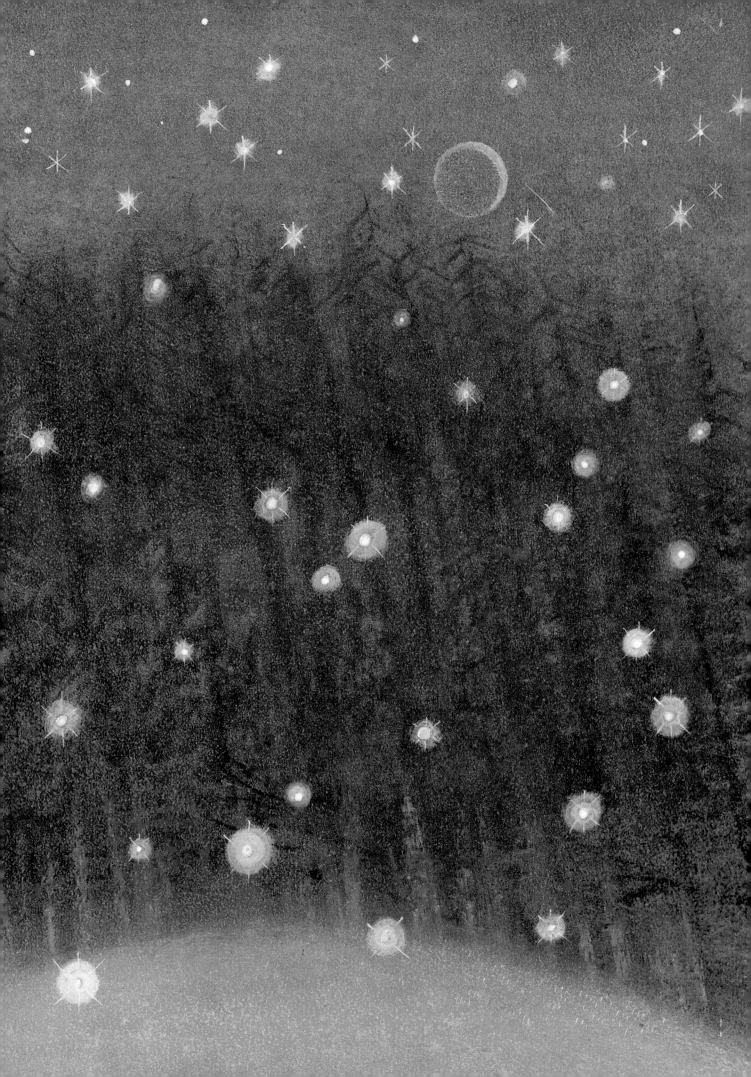

Although the little girl had given her own shirt away she found herself dressed in the finest linen. She gathered up all the coins in her skirt and was rich for the rest of her life.